Nate the Great and The Mushy Valentine

Nate the Great and The Mushy Valentine

by
Marjorie Weinman Sharmat
illustrations by Marc Simont

A Yearling Book

Published by
Yearling
an imprint of
Random House Children's Books
a division of Random House, Inc.
New York

Visit us on the Web! www.randomhouse.com/kids

Educators and librarians, for a variety of teaching tools, visit us at
www.randomhouse.com/teachers

ISBN-13: 978-0-440-41013-3
ISBN-10: 0-440-41013-4
Reprinted by arrangement with Delacorte Press
Printed in the United States of America
One Previous Edition
December 2004
35

For my two Nates:

For you, my grandson,
Nathan Sharmat,
born December 12, 1992

And in memory of your
great-grandfather,
Nathan Weinman,
born one hundred years earlier
on July 12, 1892

Always remember, Nate is great!

My name is Nate the Great.
I am a detective.
I have a dog, Sludge.
He is a detective too.
He helps me with my cases.
But one day I had to help
Sludge with his case.

It was Valentine's Day.
Sludge was napping
in his doghouse.
I tiptoed up to it.
I saw a big red paper heart
taped to the outside of the house.
Something was printed on the heart.
I LOVE YOU SLUDGE
MORE THAN FUDGE.
Someone had given Sludge
a valentine!
I was glad that no one had given me
a valentine.
I, Nate the Great, do not like
mushy words.
Or slushy words.
I, Nate the Great, do not want to be
anyone's valentine.

Sludge came out of his doghouse.

I showed him his valentine.

It was signed with initials.

ABH.

"Who is ABH?" I asked Sludge.

Sludge sniffed the valentine.

And sniffed it.

He did not know who it was from, either.

He looked at me.

"You want me to help you
find out who sent you
this valentine?" I asked.
"This is not my kind of case."
But Sludge is my kind of dog.
I wrote a note to my mother.

Dear Mother,
I am on a Valentine case.
Somebody loves Sludge
more than fudge.
When I find out who
I will be back.
Love,
Nate the Great

Sludge and I looked for
footprints around his doghouse.
Sludge carried his valentine
in his mouth
while he looked.
He liked it.
We did not see any footprints.
I was thinking,
What clues do I have?

The printing on the valentine
was made with stencils.
Anybody could have done it.
And anybody could have
stuck the valentine
on the doghouse.
Who do Sludge and I know?
We know Rosamond, Oliver, Claude,
Annie, Annie's little brother Harry,
Esmeralda, Pip, and Finley.
None of them have the initials ABH.
I saw Annie and her dog, Fang,
coming toward us.
Fang will never be anybody's
valentine.
"I have a case for you," Annie said.
"I can't find a valentine that I made.
Please look for it."

"I already have a valentine case,"
I said. "Somebody gave Sludge
a valentine, but we don't know who.
I, Nate the Great,
take only one case at a time."
"I must find my valentine,"
Annie said. *"Please."*
I wrote another note to my mother.

Dear Mother
Two Valentine cases.
I will be back.
Love,
Nate the Great

"Tell me about your missing
valentine," I said to Annie.
"This morning Rosamond and I each
made a valentine at my house,"
Annie said. "Rosamond called them
valentwins."
"Valentwins?"
"Yes, because her valentine and my
valentine looked exactly alike.
We each cut out a big red paper heart.
We each printed I LOVE YOU
on our hearts."
"Then what happened?" I asked.
"Rosamond went home with
her valentine,"
Annie said. "I began to sign my name
on mine. I was going to give it
to my little brother Harry.

But Fang came into my room.
He looked hungry."
I, Nate the Great,
knew that look very well.
"Fang and I went to the kitchen,"
Annie said. "I gave him some kibbles.
When I got back to my room,
my valentine was gone."

15

"Did Rosamond tell you who she was making her valentine for?" I asked.

"No," Annie said. "What does that have to do with my case?"

"Nothing," I said. "But I am on two cases at the same time. Remember?" I pointed to Sludge. "Please look at the valentine Sludge is carrying. Does that look like the ones that you and Rosamond made?"

"Yes," Annie said. "Except that there's more printed on this one. And this one also has initials. Rosamond's valentine and my valentine just said I LOVE YOU."

"But then you started to sign yours," I said.

"Yes, but I didn't get very far,"
Annie said.

"*You* may not have gotten very far,"
I said, "but Rosamond could have
printed much more on *her* valentine
when she got home. I, Nate the Great,

say that Rosamond made her
valentine for Sludge."
"Why would she do that?"
Annie asked.
"Only Rosamond knows," I said.
"Last year she made a valentine
for the man in the moon."
"So you have solved your case,"
Annie said.
"Not quite," I said.
"Sludge's valentine
was signed with the initials ABH.

Those are not Rosamond's initials. Why would she print them on her valentine? Before I solve a case, all the pieces have to fit."

"Do you have any clues in *my* case?" Annie asked.

"I don't know. Show me where your valentine was the last time you saw it." We all walked to Annie's house.

We went to her room.
She pointed to her desk.
"The valentine was right here,"
she said.
I looked at Annie's desk.
There were pencils
and stencils and paste
and red paper on it.
No valentine.
Sludge was sniffing the desk.
"There are no clues
on this desk,"
I said to him.

But Sludge kept sniffing.
I peered over and under,
in back of, in front of,
and inside of things.
I could not find Annie's valentine.

"Your valentine is not in this room,"
I said. "Tell me, was anybody
in your house besides you and Fang
when your valentine disappeared?"

"Yes," Annie said. "Harry was
in his room."

"Hmm. He could have gone to your
room while you were in the kitchen."

"I suppose," Annie said. "But he
wouldn't have taken the valentine.
He knew I was going to give it to him
right after I finished signing
my name to it."

"Perhaps he was in a hurry to
have it," I said.

"No," Annie said. "Harry doesn't like
valentines."

"Then why did you make one for him?"
I asked.

Annie smiled. "I like to give
valentines."

"So you like to give but Harry doesn't
like to get," I said. "That could be
important. Then again, it might not
be important. I must talk to Harry.
Where is he?"

Annie shrugged. "He disappeared when the valentine disappeared."

"Aha!" I said. "That could be a big clue. Where does Harry like to go?"

"He likes to go to Rosamond's house to play with her Hexes," Annie said.

"Her Hexes?"

"You know, Rosamond's cats. She has a Super Hex, a Big Hex, a Plain Hex, and a Little Hex."

"Yes," I said. "Rosamond has a Hex for all occasions."

Suddenly I, Nate the Great, thought
of something.

"I have just solved the case," I said.

"Oh, great," Annie said. "Where is
my valentine?"

"No, not your case. Sludge's case.
I have not been thinking strange enough.
If I had, I would have known that
the pieces fit. I must speak to
Rosamond."

"And look for Harry," Annie said.

I, Nate the Great, do not like
to go to Rosamond's house.
But now I had two reasons to go there.
Annie, Sludge, Fang, and I rushed
to Rosamond's house.

Rosamond was sitting on her floor,
making a strange, squishy brown
valentine. Her four cats were crawling
all over her.

"I am on two cases," I said. "I need
Harry for one and you for the other."

"Harry was here playing with my

cats," Rosamond said. "But he left.
I don't know where he went.
But I'm here. Why do you need me?"
I took Sludge's valentine
from his mouth.

I handed it to Rosamond.

"I, Nate the Great, say that you made this valentine for Sludge and signed it ABH. Those are the initials for *A Big Hex*. This valentine was from Big Hex to Sludge, right?"

"Wrong," Rosamond said. "This valentine looks like the one I made, except for the Sludge part and the initials."

"You didn't add words or initials to yours?" I asked.

"I added words," Rosamond said. "But these are not the words. Besides, I would never do a strange thing

like make a valentine
for a cat to give to a dog."
Rosamond would do even stranger
things, but I did not want to
go into that.
"I made my valentine for a
person," Rosamond said, "but
it's a secret who. Right now
I am making a valentine out of liver
for my cats. They haven't
been eating their liver lately.

29

It's too good to throw away,
so I am changing it into
something different.
Want to watch my cats
eat their valentine?"
It was time to leave.
I said to Annie, "Go to your house
and wait there,
in case Harry comes back."
Sludge and I went home.
"I have to eat pancakes,"
I said to Sludge. "I have to think.
I have to think twice as hard
as I would if I had only
one case to solve."
I made some pancakes.
I gave Sludge a bone.
I thought about Sludge's case.

Sludge is a great dog.
Everybody loves him.
Anybody could have given him
the valentine.
That was no help to me.

I thought about Annie's case.
The only person who
could have taken the valentine
meant for Harry
was Harry.
But Annie said that Harry
doesn't like valentines.
I made more pancakes.
What had I learned at
Rosamond's house?
I learned what she did with liver
that her cats didn't want.

If that was a clue, it was a strange one.
What had I learned at Annie's house?
Sludge had kept sniffing
at Annie's desk.
Where her valentine had been.
Was that a clue?
Perhaps.
But what case was it a clue for?
Sludge's case?

Or Annie's case?

Or *both*?

Did it matter?

Perhaps I could use a clue from
one case to help solve another case!

I picked up Sludge's valentine
where he had dropped it
while he chewed his bone.

There *had* to be a reason
why Sludge's valentine looked
like Annie's and Rosamond's.

But Rosamond said she had made hers
for a secret person.

And Annie said she had made hers
for her brother Harry.

I stared at the initials ABH.

I now knew they didn't mean
A Big Hex.

But they had to be *somebody's* initials.
Who would sign ABH?
Suddenly I, Nate the Great, had a lot
of pieces that fit.
"We must go back to Annie's house,"
I said.
Sludge dropped his bone and
picked up his valentine.
We went to Annie's house.

Sludge sniffed Annie's desk again.
"I have solved your case,"
I said to Annie. "See how
Sludge is sniffing your desk?
That's because *his* valentine
was once on your desk.
His valentine was *your*
valentine."

"What?" Annie said.

"How much of your name did you
print on your valentine before
you had to stop?" I asked.

"Just A," Annie said. "I was going
to finish with NNIE."

"I, Nate the Great, say that your
brother Harry saw the valentine
you made for him. He didn't want
it. So he added the words
SLUDGE MORE THAN FUDGE.
Then he added B and H to the A
you had signed. ABH stands for
Annie's Brother Harry. Then he
took the valentine to Sludge's
doghouse and stuck it there."

"But why didn't he just throw away the valentine instead of doing all of that?" Annie asked.

"For the same reason Rosamond could not throw away the liver," I said. "Remember when she told us it was too good to throw away, so she changed it into something different? Harry did not want to throw away something good, either:

the valentine you made for him.
So he changed it into something
different . . . a valentine for Sludge."
"But why Sludge?" Annie asked.
"Look how much Sludge likes it,"
I said. "Harry had a very good idea."
"I will never make another valentine
for Harry," Annie said.
"Harry will be glad to hear that,"
I said. I turned to go.
I had solved Annie's case.
I had solved Sludge's case.
They were the same case.
Sludge and I walked home.
I saw something
stuck to my front door.

It was a big red paper heart.
I had gotten a valentine after all!
I knew who it was from.
I knew what I did not want
to know.
I was Rosamond's secret person.
I walked up to the door.
I, Nate the Great,
was about to read that
Rosamond loves me.
I was not ready for that.
I would never be ready for that.
But I had to face it.
I read I LOVE YOU NATE
BECAUSE YOU'RE GREAT.
I had to take this valentine
off my door!

But if I touched it,
it would be mine.
Perhaps the valentine would fall off
by itself.
Or blow away.
Rot.
Die.

I, Nate the Great, could wait.
I stepped backward.
I knew another house
where I could wait.
Sludge was very glad to have me.

~~ Extra ~~
Fun Activities!

What's Inside

Nate snooped around the library to learn more about Valentine's Day. Here's what he uncovered.

NATE'S NOTES: Valentine's Day

People send more than a billion Valentine's Day cards each year. Most of those people are girls and women.

People also send flowers on Valentine's Day. Loads of flowers—including about 110 million roses.

4

Long ago, an emperor lived in Rome. He thought more men would be soldiers if they couldn't have families. So he banned marriage.

A man called Valentine helped people get married anyway.

The emperor got mad. He threw Valentine in jail.

Valentine fell in love with his guard's daughter. He wrote her mushy letters from jail.

Valentine's Day is probably named after this man.

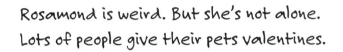

Rosamond is weird. But she's not alone.
Lots of people give their pets valentines.

The first Valentine's Day card was sent in
the year 1415.

Americans spend more than a billion
dollars on candy each Valentine's Day.

The bestselling Valentine candy?
"Sweethearts"—those tiny hearts with
words. The NECCO company has made
them since 1866. NECCO
makes about 8 billion
Sweethearts
each year.

The human mouth is just warm enough to melt chocolate.

Hershey's makes more than 80 million "Kisses" every day.

Americans buy 36 million heart-shaped boxes of chocolate every Valentine's Day.

Eating chocolate can make you feel as if you're falling in love. Yuck!

Check Your Valentine Smarts

Are you as smart as Nate? Prove it by answering these Valentine questions. It's okay to look for the answers in a book. Or check the Web.

1. When is Valentine's Day celebrated?
   a. the first Tuesday in February
   b. February 14
   c. February 15

2. Who gets the most Valentines?
   a. math teachers
   b. moms and dads
   c. dogs named Fang
   d. space aliens

3. Which of the following is not a popular Valentine's gift?
   a. liver
   b. chocolate
   c. flowers

4. Which flower is popular on Valentine's Day?
   a. red rose
   b. purple lily
   c. cactus flower

5. What does the letter X mean at the bottom
   of a valentine?
   a. buried treasure
   b. a kiss
   c. the mark of Zorro

6. Who was Valentine?
   a. an outfielder for the Yankees
   b. a man who helped Romans get married
   c. a singer

7. When do people buy the most candy?
   a. Valentine's Day
   b. Halloween
   c. Thanksgiving

8. You shouldn't give chocolate to a dog. Why?
   a. It hurts the dog's kidneys and heart.
   b. The cats will get jealous.
   c. Dogs prefer jelly beans.

9. In what country do people eat the most chocolate?
   a. The United States
   b. Switzerland
   c. Australia

10. Where is the biggest chocolate factory in the world?
    a. London
    b. Mexico City
    c. Hershey, Pennsylvania

Answers: 1. b; 2. b; 3. a; 4. a; 5. c; 6. b; 7. b; 8. a; 9. b; 10. c.

10

Valentine Riddles

What did the elephant
say to his valentine?
I love you a ton.

What did the pickle say
to her valentine?
You mean a great dill to me.

What did the octopus say
to his valentine?
*I want to hold your hand,
hand, hand, hand, hand,
hand, hand, hand.*

What did the farmer
give his valentine?
Hogs and kisses.

How to Make Love Bugs

Valentines aren't all hearts and flowers.
These look like bugs!

GET TOGETHER:

- plastic spoons
- newspaper
- ready-to-use plaster of Paris*
- a butter knife
- small magnets*
- Q-tips or paintbrushes
- paint
- glue
- wiggle eyes*

* You can buy these things in a crafts store.

HOW TO MAKE YOUR LOVE BUG VALENTINES:

1. Lay the spoons out on the newspaper.
2. Fill each spoon with plaster of Paris. Level with the butter knife.
3. Wait about 2 minutes. Press a small magnet into each spoonful of plaster of Paris.
4. Let dry completely.
5. Push on the edges of the spoons to pop out the plaster "bugs." Smooth the edges with the butter knife.
6. Using Q-tips or paintbrushes, paint the bugs red and black like real ladybugs. Or use other colors to invent new bugs.
7. Let the paint dry.
8. Glue on wiggle eyes.

Annie's Chocolate Dip Recipe

Making dip helps Annie get into the Valentine's Day spirit. (Nate prefers pancakes.)

GET TOGETHER:

- a cookie sheet
- waxed paper
- a small (6-ounce) package of chocolate chips
- a glass bowl
- strawberries, apple slices, banana slices, grapes
- a rubber spatula

HOW TO MAKE YOUR DIP:

1. Cover the cookie sheet with waxed paper.
2. Pour the chocolate chips into the glass bowl.
3. Microwave on high for 30 seconds.

4. Using oven mitts, remove the bowl from the microwave. Stir the chips with the rubber spatula.
5. Microwave on high for another 30 seconds. Remove. Stir.
6. Repeat until the chocolate just BEGINS to melt. Be careful not to let it get too hot.
7. Stir until the lumps disappear. If you need to, microwave for a few more seconds. Let the chocolate cool for a minute.
8. Dip the fruit into the cooled melted chocolate. Place on the waxed paper.
9. Set aside for about 2 hours, until the chocolate gets hard.
10. Eat!

More Valentine Riddles

What did the stamp say to the envelope?
Stick with me and we'll go places.

What travels around the world but stays in one corner?
A stamp.

What does an envelope say when you lick it?
It shuts up.

Knock
knock.
Who's there?
Olive.
Olive who?
Olive you!

Jell-O Hearts Recipe

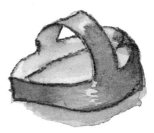

Jell-O hearts are a nice snack
to have while making valentines.

GET TOGETHER:

- 2 large boxes of strawberry or cherry Jell-O
- 2½ cups of boiling water
- unflavored cooking spray
- a large rectangular pan
- a spatula
- a heart-shaped cookie cutter

HOW TO MAKE YOUR JELL-O HEARTS:

1. Pour the Jell-O powder into a bowl.
2. Add the boiling water.
3. Stir until the Jell-O dissolves completely.
4. Spray the pan lightly with the cooking spray.
5. Pour the Jell-O into the pan.
6. Chill the pan in the refrigerator for at least 3 hours.
7. Cut out Jell-O hearts with the cookie cutter.
8. Lift the hearts from the pan with the spatula. Place on a pretty plate and serve to your valentine.

Still More Valentine Riddles

Knock knock.
Who's there?
Justin.
Justin who?
Just in time! Here's your valentine.

Knock knock.
Who's there?
Arthur.
Arthur who?
Arthur any
chocolates left
for me?

Knock knock.
Who's there?
Oscar.
Oscar who?
Oscar if she likes me!

How to Make a
Puppy Love Pendant

Sludge liked his valentine. Maybe your pet would like one, too. Here's an easy one to make.

GET TOGETHER:

- cardboard
- scissors
- a hole punch
- colored markers
- clear Con-Tact paper*
- a small metal ring*

* You can find these things in a hardware or crafts store.

HOW TO MAKE YOUR PENDANT:

1. Cut a heart shape out of your cardboard.
2. Punch a hole in the top.
3. Use markers to decorate the heart. Write your pet's name. Or try "Poodle Power" or "Cats Rule."
4. Cover the heart on both sides with the clear Con-Tact paper.
5. Trim the Con-Tact paper to the same size as your heart.
6. Clip the heart onto your dog or cat's collar with the small metal ring.

How to Make a Grass Heart

Here's another valentine you can make.

GET TOGETHER:

- a pen
- a heart-shaped cookie cutter
- a new sponge
- scissors
- grass seed
- a clean spray bottle
- water
- plastic wrap
- a red plastic plate

HOW TO MAKE YOUR GRASS HEART:

1. Use the pen and the cookie cutter to trace a heart shape onto the sponge. Cut out the shape.
2. Rinse the sponge. Let dry.
3. Put the sponge inside the cookie cutter. Place on a plastic plate.
4. Sprinkle grass seed on the sponge. Spray the seed lightly with water. Cover with plastic wrap.
5. When shoots appear, remove the plastic wrap.
6. Remind your valentine to spray with water every day. Your valentine can also "mow" his or her heart with scissors.

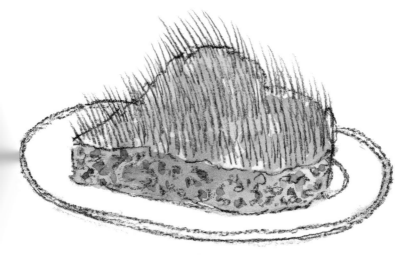

Mailing a Valentine

Almost a billion valentines are mailed each year! How do all those cards get where they're going? Read on to find out.

PARTS OF AN ENVELOPE

THE
RETURN
ADDRESS
tells the post office where to send the letter if it can't be delivered.

Rosamond Strange
Four Hexes Place
Clues, Maine 04130

THE STAMP *pays to have the letter delivered. The United States Postal Service prints special heart stamps for Valentine's Day.*

THE ADDRESS: *The first line of the address is the name of the person who will get the card. The second line should include the person's house number and street. Next line: city, state, and zip code.*

THE ZIP CODE *is a code with five numbers. It helps postal workers sort the mail.*

Nate the Great
24 Sleuth Street
Clues, Maine 04130

How Valentines Travel

STEP ONE: You mail a valentine by dropping it in a collection box.

STEP TWO: A postal employee picks up all the letters in the box. He or she delivers them to the local post office.

STEP THREE: Sacks of mail from all over the area are dumped onto a moving belt.

STEP FOUR: A machine prints lines on the stamps so they can't be used again. Each piece of mail gets a postmark. A postmark shows the date and the place where the letter was mailed.

STEP FIVE: Using the zip codes, machines and postal workers sort the mail.

STEP SIX: Letters going to different areas are trucked to the nearest airport. They take a plane ride to get where they're going.

STEP SEVEN: Mail carriers sort the mail for their routes.

STEP EIGHT: Mail carriers deliver the mail on foot or in a car or truck. Your valentine picks up his or her mail—and gets a special message. Happy Valentine's Day!

Have you helped solve all Nate the Great's mysteries?

☐ **Nate the Great**: Meet Nate, the great detective, and join him as he uses incredible sleuthing skills to solve his first big case.

☐ **Nate the Great Goes Undercover**: Who—or what—is raiding Oliver's trash every night? Nate bravely hides out in his friend's garbage can to catch the smelly crook.

☐ **Nate the Great and the Lost List**: Nate loves pancakes, but who ever heard of cats eating them? Is a strange recipe at the heart of this mystery?

☐ **Nate the Great and the Phony Clue**: Against ferocious cats, hostile adversaries, and a sly phony clue, Nate struggles to prove that he's still the greatest detective.

☐ **Nate the Great and the Sticky Case**: Nate is stuck with his stickiest case yet as he hunts for his friend Claude's valuable stegosaurus stamp.

☐ **Nate the Great and the Missing Key**: Nate isn't afraid to look anywhere—even under the nose of his friend's ferocious dog, Fang—to solve the case of the missing key.

❏ **Nate the Great and the Snowy Trail**: Nate has his work cut out for him when his friend Rosamond loses the birthday present she was going to give him. How can he find the present when Rosamond won't even tell him what it is?

❏ **Nate the Great and the Fishy Prize**: The trophy for the Smartest Pet Contest has disappeared! Will Sludge, Nate's clue-sniffing dog, help solve the case and prove he's worthy of the prize?

❏ **Nate the Great Stalks Stupidweed**: When his friend Oliver loses his special plant, Nate searches high and low. Who knew a little weed could be so tricky?

❏ **Nate the Great and the Boring Beach Bag**: It's no relaxing day at the beach for Nate and his trusty dog, Sludge, as they search through sand and surf for signs of a missing beach bag.

❏ **Nate the Great Goes Down in the Dumps**: Nate discovers that the only way to clean up this case is to visit the town dump. Detective work can sure get dirty!

❏ **Nate the Great and the Halloween Hunt**: It's Halloween, but Nate isn't trick-or-treating for candy. Can any of the witches, pirates, and robots he meets help him find a missing cat?

❏ **Nate the Great and the Musical Note**: Nate is used to looking for clues, not listening for them! When he gets caught in the middle of a musical riddle, can he hear his way out?

❑ **Nate the Great and the Stolen Base**: It's not easy to track down a stolen base, and Nate's hunt leads him to some strange places before he finds himself at bat once more.

❑ **Nate the Great and the Pillowcase**: When a pillowcase goes missing, Nate must venture into the dead of night to search for clues. Everyone sleeps easier knowing Nate the Great is on the case!

❑ **Nate the Great and the Mushy Valentine**: Nate hates mushy stuff. But when someone leaves a big heart taped to Sludge's doghouse, Nate must help his favorite pooch discover his secret admirer.

❑ **Nate the Great and the Tardy Tortoise**: Where did the mysterious green tortoise in Nate's yard come from? Nate needs all his patience to follow this slow . . . slow . . . clue.

❑ **Nate the Great and the Crunchy Christmas**: It's Christmas, and Fang, Annie's scary dog, is not feeling jolly. Can Nate find Fang's crunchy Christmas mail before Fang crunches on *him*?

❑ **Nate the Great Saves the King of Sweden**: Can Nate solve his *first-ever* international case without leaving his own neighborhood?

❑ **Nate the Great and Me: The Case of the Fleeing Fang**: A surprise Happy Detective Day party is great fun for Nate until his friend's dog disappears! Help Nate track down the missing pooch, and learn all the tricks of the trade in a special fun section for aspiring detectives.

❑ **Nate the Great and the Monster Mess**: Nate loves his mother's deliciously spooky Monster Cookies, but the recipe has vanished! This is one case Nate and his growling stomach can't afford to lose.

❑ **Nate the Great, San Francisco Detective**: Nate visits his cousin Olivia Sharp in the big city, but it's no vacation. Can he find a lost joke book in time to save the world?

❑ **Nate the Great and the Big Sniff**: Nate depends on his dog, Sludge, to help him solve all his cases. But Nate is on his own this time, because Sludge has disappeared! Can Nate solve the case and recover his canine buddy?

❑ **Nate the Great on the Owl Express**: Nate boards a train to guard Hoot, his cousin Olivia Sharp's pet owl. Then Hoot vanishes! Can Nate find out *whooo* took the feathered creature?